Things We Hear

Stephen Banks

Acknowledgment

When I think about gratitude, it starts with GOD. Without His grace, I wouldn't have had the strength, the clarity, or the courage to write this book. I'm not perfect by any means, but He gave me the ability to share my story, and for that, I am forever thankful.

I give my deepest thanks to my parents, who taught me the power of humility, love, and respect. They laid the foundation for the man I've become, and their lessons still guide me every day. Their wisdom echoes through every chapter of this book.

To my incredible daughters, Shanta, Candice, and Isabella, and my wonderful stepdaughter, Sarah: thank you for your love, your laughter, and your creative eye. You helped me pick out the cover design, and you nailed it. Great job, ladies! Your support means more than you know.

This book took me through the ringer. It challenged me, stretched me, and made me dig deep. But through it all, my partner, my soul mate, my extraordinary wife Annette was right there beside me. She didn't just support me, she helped open my mind. She was in the trenches with me, pulling out the vision I now share with all of you. Her insight, her patience, and her belief in me made this possible.

To everyone who's been part of this journey, whether you gave advice, shared a story, or simply encouraged me, I see you, and I thank you. Everyone, this book is not just mine. It's ours.

About the Author

With years of experience officiating youth, high school, and adult league sports, Stephen has spent plenty of time in the middle of the action and the noise. He's seen the highs, the lows, and the moments that don't make the highlight reel but say everything about the game.

His writing is shaped by what he's experienced, the pressure of close calls, the sideline chatter, and the lessons that come from standing in the middle of it all. He shares what officials really deal with on the field and off offering a perspective that's often overlooked but always essential.

Whether it's a story about a rivalry game, a coach's outburst, or a quiet moment of sportsmanship, Stephen brings clarity, honesty, and a deep respect for the role officials play in keeping the game fair and keeping it going. I can't make this up!

Table of Contents

Introduction

Welcome to *Things We Hear*, a collection of my experiences and observations from over 28 years as a sports official. This book is not about criticizing anyone or any team but rather sharing insights from the perspective of an official who has witnessed the evolution of sports firsthand. As a fan, it's easy to get confused by the ever-changing rules, but as an official, staying on top of the game is crucial. Each year, new rules are added, and old ones are removed, and understanding them becomes second nature over time.

Throughout my career, I have officiated in football, basketball, and baseball, spanning various age groups and levels of competition. From youth leagues to high school, college, and semi-pro games, I have seen it all. Each level has its own set of rules and challenges, and this book aims to shed light on the unique aspects of officiating in these sports.

In the following chapters, I will share stories and anecdotes from my time on the field and court, highlighting the highs and lows, the humorous moments, and the valuable lessons learned. Whether you're a fellow official, a coach, a player, or simply a sports enthusiast, I hope you find these stories both entertaining and enlightening.

ONE

All age groups have different rules. I can only speak about the sports I've officiated football, basketball, and baseball.

I've been a football official for 28 years, a basketball official for 15 years, and a baseball official for 17 years. In football, I started with youth leagues and moved into high school, college, and semi-pro (adult league). In basketball, I officiated youth leagues and AAU up to high school. In baseball, I worked with the youth leagues and AAU up to high school and adult leagues.

Here's where it gets interesting: youth leagues (ages 6–15) have their own rules within each sport. Then you have high school rules, college rules, and professional rules. As an official, you must keep up with all these rules sets, which often change every year.

For example, in football, the rules around holding vary by level:

- In youth leagues, you cannot wrap your arms around the outside of a defensive player.

- In high school, grabbing the jersey inside the tackle box is often allowed.

- In college and the pros, you can grab the jersey of the defensive player anywhere on the field.

Teaching proper technique is essential in every sport, starting at the youth level. That's where key fundamentals are learned blocking a defender, swinging a bat, and dribbling a basketball. If coaches and parents don't teach these basics, kids will imitate what they see on TV.

During youth league games, new officials are learning alongside the kids. Veteran officials help guide both the rookies and the players. Coaching in youth leagues is volunteer-based. Some coaches know the rules; many do not. Officials must know the game and the rule book inside and out.

Ninety-nine percent of youth league coaches have their own sons or daughters on the team. Every coach wants their kid to be the star. Many get their plays from Madden Football, Xbox, PlayStation, or what they see on TV. You hear it in the huddle, kids saying, "Coach scored a touchdown with this play on Madden." When you hear play calls like "Z motion ram gold twinkle" or "mustard hotdog fly box," do you really think 7- or 8-year-olds will remember that?

Coaches should focus on teaching proper technique, or just help the kids with their homework.

Officials follow a rule book. As players get older, the game gets faster. In youth football (ages 6–8), coaches are allowed on the field. The biggest rule in this age group is that coaches must stop coaching once the center touches the ball. But you'll still see coaches calling audibles on both sides until the ball is snapped. The look on the kids' faces says it all; they have no idea what's going on.

Coaches are so competitive and focused on winning that they forget to teach fundamentals. Then you have parents pressuring coaches because their kid isn't starting or getting enough playing time. Teams often have 28 players, with the same 11 on offense and on defense. That leaves 17 kids who need to get at least one play in. The lack of playing time is what led to the rise of travel football leagues, which I'll talk about later.

While officiating a game with little kids, I once asked a coach, "Do you wish you had a helmet on?" He replied, "I'd be unstoppable!" Many coaches try to relive their glory days through their kids. They want the plays to go their way, but don't take the time to teach kids how to line up properly. We refs often help the kids line up correctly.

When 6- and 7-year-olds play, it's organized chaos. You've got eight coaches, and each one should be responsible for teaching fundamentals and helping players understand the game. It shouldn't fall on the officials to teach kids how to line up or avoid crossing the ball.

Here's an example:

Me: Coach, your players aren't on the line.

Coach: Can't you get them straight?

Me: Do I look like the coach? Do I know the play you're calling?

Coach: Then throw your flag.

Thinking back to my first game as a football referee in Hampton, Virginia, it was scary but funny. I was nervous hearing coaches and parents yelling. The parents were hostile, even early in the morning. They yelled about everything. The moms were especially vocal.

During the first and second quarters, I didn't dare throw my flag. Coaches kept shouting, "That's holding!" "That's clipping!" "That's offside!" I grew up playing football and understood the game, but all the yelling made me nervous.

After halftime, as I walked back onto the field, it was quiet. Then a strong voice shouted, "We got Mr. Magoo again!" followed by laughter from the crowd. Boy, did I feel small.

Finally, I focused on the game and threw my first flag. The whole sideline erupted in cheer, even though the penalty was against their own team. That relaxed me, and I got flag-happy after that. The team I was working with won the game, and the coach told me he had fun with me. From then on, I focused on enforcing the rule book. Coaches still questioned my calls, but things went smoothly.

I've seen great players grow up from youth leagues and make it to the pros. That's one of the greatest honors of officiating.

Top five things officials hear in all sports:

1.   "Let them play!"

2.   "Get some glasses!"

3.   "He's for the other team!"

4.   "No way!"

5.   "Are you kidding me!"

Back in the day, when a high school football game ended and officials made their way to the locker room, it wasn't always a peaceful walk. If the home team lost, especially in a close one, you could count on the losing fans to let their frustration fly. And I mean literally. Ice, soda cups, popcorn buckets, even the occasional rock came raining down like we were the villains in a movie.

That's when law enforcement started stepping in. Officials began getting escorted off the field like celebrities, minus the red carpet and applause. It wasn't about fame; it was about safety. Because when emotions run high and the scoreboard doesn't go your way, some fans forget it's just a game.

TWO

On basketball courts, you hear all kinds of things. Parents and fans are much closer to the action, and that proximity makes everything louder and more intense. Parents fuss over why their kids didn't start or complain that the coach's kid "sucks." As I mentioned before, many coaches want their child to be the star, even when their child isn't very good.

Parents yell out things like, "My son is the next Dwyane Wade, Michael Jordan," and, where I'm from, "the next Allen Iverson." All we can do as officials is chuckle, because most of those kids stink. Some have potential, but after high school, they fall off the map.

I learned quickly how seriously coaches take the game during a 10U AAU matchup. Team A was down by five points. Team B had the ball with 18 seconds left. The coach from Team A told his players to foul. Suddenly, a player from Team B shoved a player from Team A so hard that he fell to the floor. The Team B coach ran onto the court, pushed the Team A player aside, and helped his own player up. Then the Team A coach ran onto the court and shoved the Team B coach. Both coaches got into a fistfight. Assistant coaches rushed in, and we officials had to break it up. In the end, Team A won by eight points, and the parents of the two kids were fighting in the parking lot.

You have to understand the area you're in. For example, in the "hood", parents take the game seriously, hoping their child will go pro and become rich. In wealthier areas, parents don't take it as seriously, knowing their child will likely become a doctor or lawyer.

One memory stands out. During a 15U AAU scrimmage, we had three officials and about 400 people packed into a loud gym. In the first quarter, fans were yelling and dropping F-bombs, shouting things like "MF'er refs!" It was out of control. After the quarter ended, I called both head coaches and the gym coordinator over. I told them that if the game was going to continue, all fans had to leave. They had five minutes to clear the gym.

The coaches asked the coordinator if I had the authority to do that. He said yes. The coaches cleared the gym while parents fussed and cursed. Once the gym was empty, the game resumed, and it went smoothly. At the end, both coaches said it was the best decision ever. One even said he'd start doing that for his practices.

After that fight, I made it a point to talk to both coaches before every game and say, **"Good sportsmanship starts with the head coach and works its way down to the assistants, players, parents, and fans."**

One rule I was taught early on: **No game should go into overtime.** If it does, the officials probably did something wrong. In football, games can drag on. Both teams pass constantly, and every incomplete pass stops the clock. As officials, we must keep the game moving, especially when working back-to-back youth games. A youth league game should last about 90 minutes. A high school game should be around two and a half hours. When a team passes 90% of the time, it's a long day for officials.

Do officials influence the outcome of a game? Absolutely. On bang-bang plays, it's a judgment call. A foul can be called or not. A runner can be safe or out. But remember: **refs don't get paid overtime.**

In youth football, the home team provides someone to run the clock. That's a big mistake. Sometimes it's a teenager glued to their phone, missing clock starts. Other times, it's an adult who helps the home team win by not stopping the clock. If the home team is ahead, they'll let the clock run when it should stop.

From JV down to youth leagues, the clock should be kept on the field by an official. To keep games on schedule, we came up with a system:

- Each quarter = 15 minutes running clock

- Stops only for timeouts and injuries

- Halftime = 10 minutes

- Total game time = 1 hour, 10 minutes

When you have six youth games back-to-back starting at 9 a.m., you hope to be done by 5 p.m., but sometimes it runs longer. At least the cash isn't bad. Some football associations assign two or three games per day, but it's still an all-day affair. Some areas even schedule weekday games to make up for rainouts.

Friday night high school games can be a headache. You've got 12-minute quarters and a 12-minute halftime. That's 48 minutes of play and 12 minutes of break, one hour total. But with all the passing, incomplete passes, and six timeouts per team, the game can stretch to two hours and ten minutes or more.

High school games vary by area and state. Some clock operators have been doing it for 15 years or more. But even then, if they're from the home team, they might shave time off the clock to help their team win. It never fails, someone's yelling, "Why is the clock stopped?" or "Why is the clock running?" Coaches always assign a coach to watch the clock, especially in close games.

Back in the day, we had a 25-second play clock. Now it's 40 seconds, and it can be kept on the field by an official or in the end zones. If an official keeps it on the field, we have the advantage of stretching it out. But coaches will still yell, "How much time do they get?"

Some areas assign an official to run the clock. That keeps games on time and lets us leave at a decent hour.

From Little League to high school, officials can make or break a game. College and pro levels have replay, which makes it easier to get the call right. But down here, it's all judgment and all pressure.

THREE

During our monthly officials' meetings, we cover a wide range of topics. One of the main topics is coaches who whine constantly, use foul language, or simply get in our way. The more they complain, the less they seem to understand the sport. High school coaches criticize officials all the time unless they're winning.

When we review game videos, we see the mistakes officials make. But we also see the great calls we make, calls that coaches often claim were wrong. We also discuss player ejections for fighting, kicking, using racial slurs, and yes, even spitting.

In youth football leagues, coaches should study the rule books, but many don't. They rely on what they see on TV or remember from when they played "back in the day." Officials, on the other hand, must study the rule books and use them as their guide. Yet they're constantly challenged and harassed by coaches.

High school officials are required to take a test. The National High School League (NHSL) administers a yearly exam to potential officials. A passing score is 75%, though each state sets its own standards. In Virginia, the test has 75 questions; Maryland has 100. In West Virginia, you're required to take two 100-question tests.

Of the 50 states, only two, Texas and Connecticut, use college rules for high school games. Texas football (don't believe the hype) isn't superior to any other state. Yes, they have seven officials on the field, but they use college rules. Virginia and Maryland also use seven officials. West Virginia requires seven officials for regular-season, playoff, and championship games. However, in the association I belonged to, we only had five officials on the field. On rare occasions when we had six, then we were laughed at because we weren't used to it and looked like the "six stooges" out there. Funny how that same association always wondered why we never got playoffs or state championship games.

After officiating in four different states and being part of five different associations, I've learned a lot. I know which associations can help move you up to the college level. Once I got to West Virginia, my passion for officiating faded. The caliber of football wasn't what I was used to. I continued because I loved the sport and enjoyed the side hustle.

Officiating in Texas was fun and enjoyable. Some areas had Division I talent, though the region I worked in didn't. Southern Virginia took football seriously and had several D1-caliber athletes. Maryland had good athletes, too, especially at private schools. Some private schools had 14 to 15 D1 players.

High school sports should prepare you for the next level, whether as a player or an official. When states only use five officials, things get missed. With every team in shotgun formation and passing frequently, five officials simply can't see it all. At one game, the referee didn't see a defender hit the wide receiver but saw the WR retaliate, so he flagged the WR for unsportsmanlike conduct. When we reviewed the film, we saw that both players should've been penalized. The ref admitted, "I'm human, and I missed it." In college or the pros, that kind of mistake could result in a fine.

Some teams have anywhere from 7 to 20 coaches on the sideline. Really, 20 coaches! Each one was yelling something different into the officials' ears. The things we hear are a lot of buzzing. That's why you find the head coach and communicate only with him. The problem is, head coaches often tell 4 or 5 assistants to yell at the officials to distract them.

As a wing official, you make it clear: only a player on the field or the head coach can call a timeout. In college and pro games, you'll see the head coach sprinting down the sideline to call one. In high school, offensive and defensive coordinators try to call timeouts. You have to confirm with the head coach. It all comes back to which coaches actually read and understand the rules. Some referees will grant a timeout just because they heard someone yell for it.

From high school to youth leagues, assistant coaches will do everything they can to distract officials asking questions and testing your knowledge. At one high school game, we had six officials. I was the deep judge. A second-year ref was on my side, and the coach knew it. He got in her ear, looked down at me, gave a wink, and went back to distract her. Needless to say, that was her last year. After a while, you learn to tune the coaches out.

As I mentioned, officials must take a test every year to stay certified. We just wish coaches had to take one too. If they did, I guarantee there'd be a lot fewer of them on the sidelines. Because here's the truth: just because you *played* the game doesn't mean you *know* the game. But try telling that to a coach.

I've heard this line from head coaches for the last 15 years:

Coach: "Are you watching the same game I am?"

Me: "Can you believe the horrible play calling from the coach?"

Coaches are quick to belittle you or act superior. But it feels good when you get them off your back and confuse them at the same time.

As an official, you get to watch kids grow from youth leagues to high school, sometimes even to the pros. It's exciting to follow their journey. Over time, players get to know the officials. They know who's good, likable, or bad.

Parents invest thousands of dollars into sports training, hoping their child will earn a college scholarship. In many cases, especially when fathers are actively involved, families spend between $15,000 and $20,000 over nine years. This investment spans across all sports and typically includes:

1.   Travel league fees

2.   Specialized training

3.   Equipment and gear

4.   Uniforms

And after all that, some kids still don't receive a scholarship or even go to college. It's heartbreaking. Some parents even take out loans, convinced their child will make it to the pros.

The reality? Only a tiny fraction ever does. The dream is powerful, but the odds are steep.

FOUR

Sample test questions…… True or False

1) Targeting is an act by any player who takes aim and initiates contact against an opponent above the shoulders with the helmet, forearm, hand, fist, elbow, or shoulders.

2) The NFHS Football Rules Committee approved the expanded use of communication devices by coaches, players, and non-players, but the use of communication devices by players except during conferences outside the 9-yard marks continues to be prohibited.

3) The penalty for both offensive and defensive pass interference fouls is 15 yards plus a loss of down.

4) All line-to-gain and down-indicator rods must have flat lower ends covered by a protective cap.

5) If a double foul occurs during a down, the number of the next down is not the same as that of the down on which the foul occurred.

6) The goal shall be positioned with the inside edge of the crossbar in the same vertical plane as the inside edge of the end line.

7) If a low scrimmage kick is touched by R1 in the neutral zone, kick-catching interference restrictions have ended, and no fair catch can be made.

8) A football jersey must completely cover the shoulder pads and all pads worn above the waist on the torso.

9) The penalty for targeting an opponent is 10 yards.

10) The penalty for failure to properly wear mandatory equipment during the down is a loss of 10 yards, succeeding spot enforcement.

You can find the answers in the back of this book:

When a coach gets in a ref's ear, the ref must always remain calm.

CALM: not showing or feeling nervousness, anger, or other emotions.

Here are some of the consequences during a game when a coach starts cussing:

- In a youth league, a **flag** is thrown

- In high school: anything goes, except the **F-bomb**

- In college: anything goes

- In the pros: anything goes

Oh, we hear players cussing at each other all the time. When a youth player knows you heard them, they always say, "My bad."

During a youth football game, a coach didn't like a clipping call. He yelled, "That was not a clip!" Then a kid shouted, "That was bullshit!" I heard it, threw the flag, and sent him to the coach. Of course, the coach asked, "What'd he do?" I said, "He was running his mouth and cussing." Two plays later, the coach came back and said the kid claimed he didn't cuss. I laughed and said, "I wouldn't have thrown the flag if he didn't." The coach shook his head and said, "Come on, man…" This was the same coach who had been cussing throughout the game.

In another game, a kid was tackled for a 3-yard loss. The defender walked away saying, "Not in my house," and the runner shouted, "F*** you!" loud enough for the whole sideline to hear. A flag was thrown. Again, the coach asked, "What did he do?" But it gets better, the parent yelled, "Not my kid!" As an official, all you can do is shake your head.

Youth football players cuss at each other when they're losing or when a play doesn't go right. In basketball and baseball, you hear players mumble and give officials the stare-down. When basketball players drive to the basket, they always yell "AND ONE!" When I give it to them and they miss the free throw, I say, "MISS ONE!" If I don't give it to them, I say, "Toughen up!"

Parents shout wild things like:

- "Where's the foul?"

- "Why are you out of shape?"

- "I see you've never refereed a game before!"

Oh, the things we hear.

Then you get the hard-headed players, the ones who showboat and imitate what they see on TV: slamming the ball, dancing in the end zone, spinning the ball. From youth league to high school, players copy what they see. When a ref corrects them, they ask why they can't do it. The ref tells them, "Read the rules."

I was the white hat at a travel league football game. Right before the coin flip, I went over to the head coach of the green team. I asked him to call over number 23 and told him he had to remove the tinted/mirror visor on his helmet. The coach started yelling that the player had worn it all year. I explained, "I'm not worried about what happened before today."

The coach tried to outtalk me. Other coaches joined in, saying, "You refs change the rules every week." Then the boy's mother started yelling that he had worn it last week with no problem and had a doctor's note. I pulled the head coach aside and said, "Coach, we're going by National Federation of High School (NFHS) rules, right?" He said yes. I asked, "Your league doesn't have any exceptions for tinted visors, right?" He said no.

As a ref, I always carry the rule book. I pulled it out and read the rule:

"Only eye shields which are clear, without the presence of any tint, may be worn. A physician cannot supersede this rule without written consent from the state association."

Their youth league rules said nothing about tinted/mirror visors. The head coach still tried to convince me. I told him, "We're already 20 minutes late starting this game." Then the rude comments started from coaches, parents, players, and fans. I dusted myself off, stuck to the rules, and the game went on.

Before the next game, the head coach of the next game team came up to me and said, "All tinted eye shields are off for my team."

Currently, most youth leagues allow tinted/mirror visors. But when players get to high school, **only clear visors are allowed.** It's crazy that parents let their kids wear tinted/mirror visors, knowing that any kid can get a **concussion.** Guess they didn't see the movie *Concussion* with Will Smith. Are the youth kids being set up for failure?

At another youth game, during the coin flip, a few kids came out with **aluminum foil on their teeth.** Wait, what? Yes, aluminum foil. I approached the coach and asked if he knew some kids were wearing foil on their teeth. He shook his head and asked the kids why they did it. I walked away as he scolded them.

As a ref, I tell high school players all the time: "Cover your back flap or pull your pants down to cover your knees." Wide receivers love to hike their pants above their knees. But the NFHS rule states:

"The pants must cover the knee completely."

During Labor Day weekend, several high school football games air on ESPN. Most feature elite teams. The head coach must verify to the referee before the game that "his players have been issued all required equipment and will not use illegal equipment." Yet coaches let players come out dressed any kind of way. Why are the officials not enforcing these rules?

This issue won't go away until game officials take appropriate action. If NFHS fined referee associations and high schools for rule violations, maybe coaches and officials would start enforcing them.

Sports associations collect dues from officials. If you have 100 members and each pays $70+, you have the funds to cover fines. So, it's not like the association can't afford it. If it's part of the rules, **enforce it.**

As many players say, "Some officials don't care and just don't enforce it."

Pants not covering the knees are illegal in youth and high school football. Coaches need to take responsibility and teach players about safety. Once a player gets hurt, parents start looking for a payday, ready to sue anyone and everyone the hungry lawyers can go after.

The NFHS rulebook clearly outlines standards for **illegal and improperly worn player equipment** in high school football. These rules are designed to protect players and ensure fairness across all levels of competition.

Illegal equipment refers to items that are strictly prohibited, including:

- Jewelry

- Tinted visors

- Non-compliant eye shade

- Bands worn around the upper arm, neck, or legs

- Uncovered back pads

- Sweatbands and uniform adornments (including towels) that do not conform to the rules

Improperly worn equipment, on the other hand, includes gear that is legal but not worn as intended. Examples include:

- Pants not covering the knees

- Tooth and mouth protectors not worn at the start of play

- Shoulder pads not properly covered by the jersey

Wearing equipment incorrectly can reduce its protective effectiveness and increase the risk of injury.

While enforcement may be inconsistent at the college level, the NFHS is proud of the efforts made by high school players, coaches, and officials to uphold these standards. These rules are often overlooked by casual spectators, but they play a critical role in maintaining safety, fairness, and team uniformity. Despite negative influences from higher levels of play, coaches and officials must remain vigilant in enforcing equipment rules at the high school level.

Non-compliance can lead to several penalties:

- Removal of a player for one play due to improperly worn equipment.

- An unsportsmanlike conduct penalty on the head coach if players are illegally equipped after pre-game certification.

Chronic violations of equipment rules can disrupt the pace of play and compromise fairness. Repeated offenses not only endanger individual players but also affect the integrity of the game. The NFHS provides several administrative options to address persistent infractions:

- A **delay-of-game penalty** for repeated violations that slow downplay.

- An **unsportsmanlike conduct foul** under Rule 1-5-3c (10) and 9-8-1h for equipment not worn as intended.

- A head coach who fails to support these rules may also be penalized for unsportsmanlike behavior.

Coaches play a pivotal role in preventing chronic violations. They must consistently reinforce the importance of proper equipment use and educate their players. Creating a culture of accountability among teammates can also help reduce infractions.

Game officials must remain alert and enforce penalties consistently. Temporary removals and escalating consequences for repeated offenses are necessary to preserve the integrity of the sport.

High school football's equipment rules reflect the sport's commitment to **player safety and team unity**. This unity goes beyond appearance; it reinforces the idea that every player is part of a larger whole, working toward a common goal. When no player stands out for the wrong reason, the team's integrity is preserved.

While these rules may seem minor, they play a significant role in reducing injuries and maintaining the fairness and spirit of the game.

FIVE

During any game, coaches will yell just about anything when they're losing. When the game is close, a coach is looking for anything questionable on the other team to have the edge. But when it's a blowout, the losing coach just wants the game to end. Sometimes, they'll agree to shorten the quarters from 12 minutes to 10 or even less. Other times, you'll get a coach who refuses to give up, tries to rally the fans, and starts blaming the officials.

I once officiated a high school game where the team had a record of 0–28. By the third quarter, the score was already 45–0. The losing head coach kept yelling, "The refs won't throw their flags!" After the game, a mom shouted out, "The referees are cheaters!" I turned to her and said, "Your team's record is 0–28. How can we be cheating?" And believe it or not, they brought that same head coach back the next season. Sad to say, he was fired mid-season after going 0–36.

Officials don't always get it right, coaches make bad play calls, and players drop the ball. When I officiate high school and youth league games, and a coach makes a bad call or a player drops a pass, I joke and tell them to throw their red flag, the do-over flag!

I've seen so many players drop touchdown passes in the end zone, and yet coaches still blame the officials. Here's what happened at a game:

Coach: "You missed the grab on my player!"

Me: "Are you talking about before or after he dropped the pass while wide open?"

Coach: "It happened while he was running down the field."

Me: "So the defender fell and that somehow caused your player to drop the ball?"

At a game one evening, a coach approached me and asked, "When are you going to throw your flag?" I nodded in agreement. At that time, his team was on offense. Next play: false start. Then, there was an illegal substitution (12 players on the field). There were not enough players on the line (only 10 on the field). Then, after another false start, I heard another coach say to him, "Be careful what you ask for." That team could've been penalized on every play. Sometimes, to keep the game moving, we refs do what we have to do.

Too often, officials let things slide. In youth league and high school football, baseball, and basketball, you could honestly throw a flag on every single play if you wanted to. In football? There's always a hold, a false start, or someone lined up wrong. In baseball? You can open up your strike zone like a drive-thru window or tighten it like a locked vault. In basketball? You can let fouls go, ignore traveling, and pretend the 3-second rule is just a suggestion.

It's a balancing act. Call everything, and the game drags on forever. Let too much go, and chaos takes over. Officials walk that line every game, trying to keep it fair, keep it moving, and keep their sanity intact.

It never fails, there's always that one parent in the stands trying to coach from the bleachers, hyping their kid up like it's Game 7 of the NBA Finals:

Parent:

"Score more!"

"Don't pass him the ball, he's trash!"

"If you don't win this game, forget about those new Nikes!"

"Put the team on your back!"

"Show them what you're made of!"

"They're not on your level!"

"We didn't drive three hours and skip lunch for you to lose!"

Meanwhile, the kid's just trying to remember the play and tie his shoes.

One of the most memorable moments I've had was during a varsity football game. The head coach had the NFHS rule book tucked in his back pocket. At one point, he called a timeout, pulled out the book, and showed us exactly where we'd made a mistake on a call. The white hat looked at it and said, "Well, we missed it." The coach responded, "You've got to know the rules, you could cost a team the game."

I ended up officiating several more of his games, and every time, he reminded me: "I never leave home without my rule book." That kind of dedication earns respect. He didn't just coach, he knew the game inside and out.

Here's a funny one: during an NFL game, a head coach turned to the ref and said, "Hey, you know what NFL stands for?" Ref: "No, what?" Coach: "Not For Long!" Sure enough, that coach was gone the next season. Guess he was right.

At any level, a referee can change the outcome of a game. Just ask the Saints, everyone remembers that infamous no-call. The side judge had the angle. The line judge saw it too. It was as clear as day. When something that obvious gets ignored, you start to wonder: Was there a grudge? A little personal payback?

And to make it even more suspicious, that same side judge had officiated another one of their games earlier that season. Coincidence? Maybe. But I wouldn't be surprised if that ref quietly retired the next year before the pitchfork came out.

SIX

These days, youth travel leagues are everywhere, and they're a big mess. Parents pay a lot of money, thinking their kid is a superstar. Coaches stack their teams, thinking they'll win every game until they play out of state and get crushed. Some teams pay $500–$700 to enter a tournament, only to get blown out.

I once officiated a game between two all-Black teams. The white ref working the middle turned to me and said, "They're all using the N-word. What do I do?" I shrugged and said, "Let them play and we'll get paid at the end."

That game? I heard the N-word over 500 times. When a Black team is winning, you're their best friend. When they're losing, suddenly you're the enemy. They'll curse you out, call you every name in the book, and act like losing isn't even an option. And when they do lose, the coaches tell the players, "The refs cheated." Really? That's why you lost 49–0?

Here's another classic youth league issue: a team has 27 players, but only seven show up to practice all week. Then game day rolls around, and all 27 show up, and the seven who actually practiced don't even get to play. Yeah, parents notice. And they're not happy and talk.

In one game, I threw a flag for five men in the backfield. Suddenly, 20 coaches for a team with only 15 players started yelling, "Who? Where?" It was chaos. During a timeout, a woman filming the game spoke up: "It was five in the backfield." A few coaches turned and said, "Oh, okay." Just like that, the noise died down.

Sometimes, all it takes is one voice of reason with a camera to calm the storm.

In another championship game, a Black team was playing a mixed team. The Black team was losing, and the other team was driving. The Black players started complaining about the refs: "They always cheat us." "I'm never coming back to this area." "They make up stuff to cheat."

I told them to knock it off and keep quiet.

Player: "I'm talking to my teammates."

Me: "Keep the comments to yourself."

Player: "This is a f***ing joke." I threw the flag.

I went over to the coach and told him to get his players under control.

Coach: "You refs are soft!"

Me: "It's not about being soft. Your players don't have discipline. One of them just cussed you out and told you to kiss his ass, and I'm soft?"

When the coach is also the parent of a player, things can get really interesting, especially when that player takes a hit and comes up with tears in his eyes.

Scenario 1: The Protective Parent-Coach

Coach/Parent: "Son, what's wrong?"

Player: "Nothing."

Coach/Parent: "Hey ref, they're hitting my son too hard."

Ref: "It's football."

Coach/Parent: "I know, but can you keep an eye on it?"

Translation: "Please bubble-wrap my kid until halftime."

Scenario 2: The Tough-Love Parent-Coach

Coach/Parent: "Son, what's wrong? Get tough, or I'm pulling you out. Your sister hits harder than that!" Translation: "Tears are weakness. And your sister's undefeated."

Another game I officiated: Team A was up 52–6. It was the fourth quarter, running clock, and Team A had the ball on Team B's 8-yard line. With just 12 seconds left, Team A's coach called a timeout, just to score again.

I didn't grant it.

The coach lost his mind. He called me every dirty word in the book, and two of his assistants had to hold him back. I just walked away laughing and asked, "This is how you teach sportsmanship?"

Then his father came over to our tent to say something. Honestly, if it hadn't been raining and if I hadn't had a little self-control, I might've backhanded him. That coach loves running up the score on weaker teams. But when someone does it to him? He wants to fight.

He's a bully, 6'3", 250 lbs., and thinks he's the second coming of Bill Belichick. I laugh every time his team gets beat and he flips the same sideline table like it's WWE.

This kind of chaos is exactly why it's so hard to find referees for youth sports. How many fights break out across the country over kids' games? How many tragic stories have we heard over a score, a call, or a tournament trophy?

And the worst part? The same bad coaches come back year after year. That one coach who lost his mind on the sideline? They let him return the next season, and, surprise, he acted like a jerk all over again.

Facts:

- 90% of travel football teams have no Coach Code of Ethics or Conduct

- Every year, youth coaches across all sports are charged with fighting or worse

- 60% of youth coaches have gone after sports officials

- 40% of youth parents have done the same. When referees need a police escort just to get to their car after a youth game, something is seriously broken.

And don't get me started on background checks. Most leagues run cheap local checks that don't even touch state or national records. That's like locking your front door and leaving the windows wide open.

When I officiated travel league football, I didn't step on the field unless I was paid **$150 per game**. For tournaments, it's **$100 per game**. With all the nonsense we put up with, at least I was getting paid.

Every year, you hear about fights on the football fields that end in someone getting shot or worse.

The competition is intense. Parents are chasing dreams through their kids, hoping they'll be the next Michael Jordan, Michael Vick, or some future pro. It's always the same line: **"You refs are cheating the kids!"**

They'll drive three hours for a basketball game. Two hours for a football game. And if their kid doesn't win? Somebody's getting blamed.

SEVEN

There's nothing like the atmosphere before a college game, tailgates everywhere, the smell of burgers in the air… and yeah, sometimes the unmistakable scent of weed too. College football is a different beast. The players are two sizes bigger and twice as fast. If your head is not on a swivel and you're not paying attention, you'll get knocked on your butt real quick.

I worked as a back judge, which kept me in the middle of the field. My referee buddies on the sidelines had to manage the chaos with the coaches, keeping the sideline tight. No matter how tight it was, coaches always found a way to put their two cents in.

One game, I threw my flag so hard it traveled a full 20 yards for a holding call. The head coach looked at me, wide-eyed, and said, "How'd you even see that?" We both glanced up at the jumbotron, and there it was, plain as day: his player grabbing and tackling the defender like it was a wrestling match. He just laughed. During a timeout, he asked, "You ever play quarterback? Because that flag had some serious arm strength."

As a back judge, I was always in the thick of it. Punt returners loved to talk big: "I'm taking this one to the house!" One guy actually ran 50 yards… then fumbled. Next punt, I looked at him and said, "Just fair catch it, man."

Being a back judge means you're constantly scanning for deep passes, offensive and defensive pass interference, holding, blindside blocks, you name it. The action never stops, and neither do the surprises.

College coaches are all smiles before kickoff, handshakes, small talk, maybe even a joke or two. But once the game starts? They turn into drill sergeants with whistles. I saw one coach absolutely unload on a player for a facemask penalty like the kid had just cost him a national title. Another player leaned over and said, "You don't want to cross that coach." He wasn't kidding.

At the college level, you've got to be sharp. In one game, I recognized a player from the youth league. He went out for a pass, got tangled up with the defender, and I tossed the flag. Yeah, I helped him out. Sue me, I've got a soft spot for the hometown kids. After the game, we met up and told each other we were happy about moving up in the ranks.

College coaches don't mess around. If you blow a call, they'll send film to your supervisor before you've even packed up your whistle. But most of the time, they're more mad at their players than the officials. They know the rulebook, so the games usually run smoothly. Occasionally, a player will ask something completely out of left field, but most college coaches stay locked in on the game, not the refs.

Now, back to high school football. I had a game in Maryland where the head coach was yelling from the sideline, accusing me of being a graduate of the rival high school. At halftime, we officials had a good laugh about it. I told a few of his assistants, "Let him know I'm not from around here, I don't care who wins. I'm from the 757, Hampton Roads." One coach chuckled and said, "Oh, you're from the 757? That's where they play real football!"

Two weeks later, I was scheduled to ref that same team again. The head coach told my commissioner he didn't want me anywhere near his games. My commissioner's response? He assigned me to the game of the week. I appreciate that, coach! That same head coach lost again without me there and tried to scratch two more refs from his schedule. We had another good laugh over that one, too.

In West Virginia high school football, coaches can scratch a ref from their schedule for any reason. Doesn't matter if it's legit or just because the coach didn't like your socks. Here's the thing: coaches need to stop whining and just coach. We'll call the game fair and square.

At our officials' meetings, we talk about the new rules, how they'll change the game, and whether coaches will actually understand them. Kickoffs are always a circus, coaches love trying onside kicks, and they usually blow up.

Coaches complain. They try to get refs removed. But guess what? We just get reassigned to another game and still get paid. Some officials do play favorites, though. We remember the coaches who cussed us out… and then came back three weeks later all sweet and chatty:

Coach: "How've your games been?" "How's the wife and kids?" "You think the rain will hold off?"

Some refs will overlook a hold or a block in the back just to stay on a coach's good side. I've seen it in Maryland and West Virginia. In some places, refs won't throw a flag just to avoid getting scratched. That's when you know the coach has the ref in his back pocket. And trust me, only another official can spot when a game's being thrown.

In Texas, some coaches believe the secret to winning a state title is keeping the same group of kids together from age five all the way through high school. Down in South Texas, below San Antonio, I saw it firsthand. One high school had practice at 6 a.m., then again at 4 p.m. every single school day. And no, this wasn't preseason; it was year-round. Guess what? That strategy hasn't worked in over 40 years. Still no state title. But hey, at least they're consistent.

Even Texas basketball was wild. Teams didn't bother with layups; they just launched 3-pointers like it was a video game. One team went 8-for-35. The other team was 10-for-50. And that was just the first half!

As officials, we just want a clean, well-officiated game. But there's always that one coach or fan who thinks they know the rulebook better than we do.

In youth leagues, coaches love pulling out the "old deception" play: send in three players, have four come out, and leave one hiding in bounds to sprint downfield for a pass. The rulebook clearly says it's illegal, and it is intended to deceive. But they still argue:

Coach: "We did it last week, and no flag was thrown!"

Youth coaches just want to coach their sons and turn them into all-stars. Spoiler alert: it rarely works out. They spend more time yelling about flags than teaching the game. One time, a team lost, and the coach had a kid thank me for the loss. I said, "You're welcome. Now pay me." That coach had been at it for eight years and still hasn't won a championship.

Then you've got officials who say, "I don't do it for the money." Really? So you're out here for the joy of being screamed at by coaches, cursed out by players, and heckled by fans?

When I was taking care of my father, officiating was my only source of income. So to those refs who claim they "don't need the money," I say this: go volunteer. Let's see how long you last when the pay disappears but the abuse doesn't.

Let's talk numbers:

- Youth football: $60–$80 per game

- High school football: $80–$125 per game

- Texas: Only state where refs get a percentage from the gate $55 to $450 per game

AAU Baseball & Basketball:

- Baseball: $50 per game (plate), cash

    o 5 games Saturday + 5 Sunday = $500/weekend

    o 4 weekends = $2,000 cash

    o Year-round

- Basketball: $30 per game, 1 hour

    o 8–10 games/day on weekends

The number one rule is No overtime—ever

Adult Leagues:

- Baseball: $100–$150 per game (2 umps)

- Football: $150 per game (6 refs)

College Football (by division):

- DI: $1,000–$2,500

- DII: $300–$1,000

- DIII: $200–$800

- Basketball and baseball are similar

Pro Salaries (2024):

- NFL: $205K–$360K/year (17 games)

    o Plus playoff bonuses, Super Bowl pay

    o All expenses paid: hotel, flights, food, rides

- NBA: $150K–$550K/year (82 games)

- WNBA: $425 per game

- MLB: $235K/year

To get there, you've got to know the game, stay in shape, and attend a lot of camps. In DI college, expenses are covered. DII and DIII? You're driving yourself.

So, looking at this list below, you'll find one high school football team listed twice. To do that, you have to have a winning program.

According to stadiumtalk.com, here are the Top 5 winningest high school football coaches:

Nov. 29, 2024

1. John McKissick

- W-L record: 621-156-13
- Win percentage: .794
- Years: 63 seasons (1952-2014)
- Schools: Summerville High School (Summerville, South Carolina)
- State titles: 10 (1955, 1956, 1969, 1978, 1979, 1982, 1983, 1984, 1986, 1998)

2. John T. Curtis Jr.

W-L record: 603-75-6

Win percentage: .881

Years: 52 (1969-present)

Schools: John Curtis Christian School (River Ridge, Louisiana)

State titles: 26 (1975, 1977, 1979, 1980, 1981, 1983, 1984, 1985, 1987, 1988, 1990, 1993, 1996, 1997, 1998, 1999, 2001, 2002, 2004, 2005, 2006, 2007, 2008, 2011, 2012, 2018)

3. Mike Smith

W-L record: 506-100-2

Win percentage: .832

Years: 51 (1971-2021)

Schools: Hampton High School (Hampton, Virginia)

State titles: 12 (1975, 1977, 1980, 1981, 1985, 1986, 1988, 1995, 1006, 1997, 1998, 2005)

4. Robert Hyland

W-L record: 478-107-2

Win percentage: .814

Years: 50 (1971-present)

Schools: St. Mary's Springs Academy (Fond du Lac, Wisconsin)

State titles: 17 (1983, 1984, 1990, 1991, 1995, 1997, 1998, 1999, 2002, 2009, 2011, 2012, 2014, 2015, 2017, 2018, 2019)

5. Phil Danaher

W-L record: 490-118-4

Win percentage: .800

Years: 47 seasons (1974-2021)

Schools: Dilley High School (Dilley, Texas), Hamshire-Fannett High School (Hamshire, Texas), Calallen High School (Corpus Christi, Texas)

State titles: None

According to the Playfootball.NFL.com, here are the 2025 top 14 Winningest High School Football Programs:

No. 1 Valdosta (Georgia)	965	965-256-34
No. 2 Washington (Massillon, Ohio)	959	959-302-36
No. 3 Male (Louisville, Kentucky)	957	957-343-49
No. 4 Mayfield (Kentucky)	955	955-267-32
No. 5 Highlands (Ft. Thomas, Kentucky)	943	943-265-26
No. 6 Mount Carmel (Pennsylvania)	907	907-344-43
No. 7 Muskegon (Michigan)	903	903-294-43
No. 8 Canton McKinley (Ohio)	882	882-381-42
No. 9 Easton (Pennsylvania)	881	881-388-54
No. 10 Haynesville (Louisiana)	879	879-313-34
No. 11 Steubenville (Ohio)	874	874-334-36
No. 12 Everett (Massachusetts)	865	865-388
No. 13 Parkersburg (West Virginia)	857	857-359-33
No. 14 Hampton (Virginia)	856	856-297-43

It's no secret, from youth leagues to college sports, recruiting is everywhere. And in the pros? It's practically an art form all in the name of chasing a championship. These days, more people are looking for shortcuts to build that dream team. You'll even hear it happening right on the field or court, kids swapping phone numbers, whispering about which coach gives out the best gear or perks. When one player tells another about the "extras" they're getting, their eyes light up like it's Christmas morning.

Then come the rivalry games, where the trash talk hits another level. In high school, it doesn't stop players from carrying that same energy from football season straight into basketball. The sport changes, but the attitude stays.

And it's not just the players switching sports. Officials do it too. One week you're calling holding penalties, the next you're whistling traveling violations. Just like the athletes, we adapt, hustle, and keep the game moving no matter what field or court we're on.

In college, you won't find officials working multiple sports. At that level, most are laser-focused on one thing: moving up to the pros. It's not about variety anymore; it's about mastery. They're chasing precision, consistency, and exposure. Every game is a chance to prove they belong on a bigger stage. The grind is real, and the goal is clear: get noticed, get promoted, and earn that spot under the bright lights.

By the time athletes reach college, most of them know whether they've got what it takes to move up. That dream starts early in youth leagues filled with ambition, and parents pushing hard, sometimes too hard. But all it takes is one life-changing injury to shift everything. That's why education isn't just important, it's essential. Sports can open doors, but they don't guarantee a future. You need that backup plan. Because when the cheering stops and the lights go out, it's what you've learned off the field that helps you make it in the real world.

EIGHT

Baseball can be a quick game if you open up the strike zone. Umpires control the pace. If you've got a team that swings the bat, no problem. But weaker teams? That's a whole different story. Their eighth and ninth batters just stand there hoping for a walk like they're waiting for a bus. The older the kids, the more they swing. They know the game moves faster when you actually play it.

When dads camp out behind the backstop and start judging your strike zone, things get loud. I'm talking moans, groans, and a full-blown chorus of "COME ON!" That's when I got creative. I brought a tarp and strung it up so parents couldn't stand directly behind the plate and critique every pitch like it was Sunday Night Baseball.

The complaints came in hot:

Parents: "Here comes the idiot ump."

"What a bastard."

"Why does he keep doing that?"

"Hey, ump, your house is on fire. Go home."

"Can we ban him?"

"I hate this ump, he's a jerk."

The baseball director backed me one hundred percent and told the parents to take a seat in the stands. Two weeks later, he put up his own tarp, bigger and wider. No more backstop critics. Problem solved.

One time, I was working the field between second and third base. A runner came sliding hard into third, bang-bang play. The tag was high, his foot hit the bag first, so I called him safe.

Next thing I know, the coach comes storming out of the dugout, arms flailing like he's auditioning for a Broadway musical.

Coach: "Did you get a good look at that?"

Me: "Yes, Coach. His foot hit the bag, and the tag was high."

Coach: "Alright, I trust your judgment. I just had to come out here, so the parents think I'm doing my job. Gotta put on a show so they don't think I'm soft. You've been great at all my games. This is just for the crowd."

He turned to walk away, and just when I thought we were good, he tossed one more line over his shoulder:

Coach: "You need to get into the game and open your eyes."

That moment made me realize some coaches aren't just coaching. They're performing. And the parents? They repeat whatever they hear from the sideline like it's gospel.

During another game, a kid slid into third and came up limping. I called him out. Between innings, a parent yelled, "Take care of my investment." That was a first.

Here are some of the things we hear from parents.

"Call that foul. That's my 401K."

"My son is my meal ticket out of here."

"They can't beat up my son. He's going to the NBA."

"You refs need to understand. My son is never pulled out of the game."

"Guess you've never seen a superstar before."

I was once behind the plate at an 11-and-under AAU tournament. Team A was up 2 to 0, and one dad from Team A had a booming voice that echoed across the field. He kept yelling, "Strike three! You out! Swing, batter!" like he was auditioning for the role of stadium announcer. The moms from Team B weren't having it. They told him to shut up. He just laughed in that mocking, smug way that only makes things worse.

Fast forward to the championship game. The same two teams were playing. That loud dad started up again, even louder than before. But this time, the moms from Team B came prepared. Out of nowhere, five of them pulled out homemade noisemakers (cans filled with rocks). Every time he opened his mouth, they shook those cans like maracas at a parade. You couldn't hear a word he said. He was furious. I laughed so hard I had tears in my eyes.

Team B won the game, and those moms walked off the field in perfect rhythm, shaking their cans like a victory band.

Then there was the AAU basketball game where a parent stormed onto the court and punched an official in the face because he didn't call a foul on his kid. Another parent from the same team jumped in. Words turned into punches. Police were called. And the kids? They just stood there watching like it was part of the halftime show. These kids were only eleven years old.

AAU games can get intense. These days, they call them "club teams." Some programs fly kids in from other states just to play. And people wonder where all the money comes from. That's a whole other book.

I had another heated AAU game where the kids were trash-talking at one another.

Player A: "You're a bum."

Player B: "Don't be mad because I burned you."

Player A: "Step your game up."

Player B: "I got your game right here."

Player A: "You're weak ass."

Then the parents jumped in. Player A had a breakaway layup, and Player B fouled him hard. Player A's dad rushed down and shoved Player B, who hit the wall. Then Player B's dad came down swinging. I knew him and tried to pull him back, but the court had already turned into a boxing ring.

Police came. Game over. And all of this happened in the second quarter.

You hear the wildest things kids say on the field or court:

"Coach, I have to go to the bathroom."

"He's hitting too hard."

"My dad said I'm going to the NFL."

"Baseball's not my favorite sport."

"Why is that coach cussing?"

"That's a girl, can we hit her hard?"

"My dad makes me dribble in the house when my mom's not home."

"Can I throw your flag?"

"Our coach is an asshole."

"Our plays are from Xbox."

"Can I move the ball over here?"

"Please don't strike me out."

During a 9-to-11 age football game, a kid ran down the sideline on his team side, stepped out of bounds twice, and still scored the game-winning touchdown with 27 seconds left. The coach looked at me and said, "Thank you!" I just shook my head. And remember, there's no overtime.

Now let's talk about high school football. In the past 20 years, I've been a referee, and I've seen every team run shotgun, even from the half-yard line. I've watched this play out in playoff games, and it still blows my mind.

First and goal from the half-yard line

Shotgun snap goes back 4 yards

Handoff goes back two more

Now the ball's on the 6-yard line

Running back gets stopped at the 4-yard line

Next play: shotgun again

Ball goes back to the 8. Incomplete pass

Third down: shotgun. Pass to the wide receiver. Tackled at the 1

Fourth down: shotgun. Quarterback sacked at the 5

All it takes is the ball to break the plane of the goal line. So why run shotgun from the half-yard line? That's where football IQ comes in. Just because you played the game doesn't mean you know the game.

My high school coach used to say, "Whatever play you run in shotgun, you can run under center. And whatever play you run under center, you can run in shotgun." It's not about the formation, it's about knowing when to use it.

Team A played Team B in the regular season. Final score was 70–0. In the playoffs, they met again. Team A had a great run; the ball ended on the half-yard line. First and goal, they had four downs in shotgun. They did not score. The fans lit up the coach:

"Damn, you blew it!"

"Oh my God, when will you get it right?"

"Did you watch the tape from last game?"

"Coach, can I help you call the next play?"

"Don't blow this game!"

"Who's calling the plays, Bugs Bunny?"

The defense was lined up in the gaps; nobody over the center. It was practically an open invitation for a QB sneak under the center. But the quarterback hadn't been taught to read the defense or audible out of the play. So instead of walking into the end zone untouched, they ran the called play and got stuffed. Team B won again, 45–7.

And don't get me started on coaches who wander out of the designated area during live play. When I throw a flag, they call me petty. I just say it is in the rulebook.

Coach: "Get the other team back!"

Me: "This is my sideline."

Coach: "You need to watch the holding!"

Me: "When I see it, I'll call it."

Fan: "He never sees when they hold!"

Coach: "Why do we have 10 penalties, and they only have 1?"

Me: "Guess they're more disciplined."

Coaches worry more about missed calls than missed free throws or dropped passes. But hey, that's youth sports.

NINE

Football officiating isn't just about knowing the rules; it's about surviving the politics. Working with different associations taught me how to move up the ladder. I've been in groups with 36 members and others with over 300. Most won't let you touch a varsity game until you've got four years under your belt. But one association I joined had rookies doing varsity games right out of the gate. No experience and no clue. Just warm bodies in stripes.

Why? Because the commissioner was greedy. He wanted to cover as many schools as possible, and he got a percentage off every official's pay. He was also the game assignor, and he took another slice. During meetings, he'd tell rookies, "Don't throw your flag." So, at game time, guess what? They didn't. One rookie even left his flags in the car. Watching them work this game, I had a headache from all the confusion.

Coaches know when officials are new. And they don't hold back on them.

Coach: "This your first year on varsity?"

Official: "Yes, sir."

Coach: "Make sure you watch the end, he holds a lot."

Official: "I'll look for it."

Coach: "If you need water, just let me know."

Official: "Thanks, Coach."

End of the first quarter:

Coach: "I told you to watch the end, he's holding every play!"

Official: "I didn't see it."

Coach: "You missed it several times."

Official: "I'm on it."

End of the game:

Coach: "You cost us the game by not calling holding."

Official: "Better luck next time." Final score? 42–0.

Most associations work within their own area. But then they start creeping into other territories, undercutting each other like it's a turf war. And whenever you hear an official say, "I don't do it for the money," just know they must be doing it for the abuse. Coaches, players, and fans will let you have it when you mess up.

Learning football rules is no joke. Basketball and baseball? Pretty much what you see on TV. But football? It's a maze. Youth league and high school use NFHS rules. Then you've got Pop Warner rules. Then, area-specific rules. And don't forget travel leagues where anything goes. Coaches and parents mix it all up with college and pro rules.

Now here's a funny one. I was the white hat for a game. White hats rarely throw flags. But some parents hated me anyway.

Parent: "You're a terrible ref!"

Me: "How can I be terrible if I never threw a flag?"

Parent: "You probably told the other refs not to throw theirs so your team could win!"

Me: "We're looking for good refs like you. Do you want to apply?"

One time, I was shopping, and two parents approached me.

Father: "Hey, you're that referee!"

Me: "Huh?"

Father: "You reffed my son's game two weeks ago."

Me: "You've got me mixed up with my twin."

Mother: "Tell your twin he's a bad ref. My son said he got face-masked, and the ref didn't see anything."

Me: "Was he wearing his glasses?"

Father: "Nope. Missed a lot of holding calls, too."

Me: "People always confuse us."

Mother: "The coach said your brother's son played for the other team, that's why he cheated."

Me: (laughing) "I'll talk to my twin."

Phew, that was a close one!

I run into people all the time who say, "I couldn't do your job." One time, I saw a high school coach after the season ended. He shook his head at me. I shook mine back at him.

Ten minutes later:

Coach: "Do I pay you now or later?"

Me: "For what?"

Coach: "That game where you were the back judge, you called offensive pass interference and took away their touchdown."

Me: "He pushed off the defender."

Coach: "Next play was a fumble, and we recovered and won."

Me: "That touchdown would've tied the game."

You would be surprised how many people have tried to bribe me over the years. I've never taken one. But here's the truth: officials don't need a bribe to affect the outcome of a game. A missed call, a flag held too long, or a moment of hesitation can shift everything.

Players are supposed to respect officials. But when they see coaches and parents constantly challenging and disrespecting us, they start thinking it's a fair game. I've seen players spit at refs. I've heard "asshole" more times than I can count. One wide receiver missed a pass and called the ref a "blind bitch." That's the kind of sideline abuse we sometimes deal with.

I was the white hat during a game when Player A blocked Player B. Player B got up and shoved Player A. I threw the flag personal foul. As Player B walked to the sideline, he ripped off his helmet, threw it, and yelled, "MFing refs always cheating!" Another ref heard it and threw his flag too. The head coach looked at me and said, "He didn't mean it." I asked, "Would you let your kid say that to you?"

Football's gotten soft. We have to watch for blindside blocks and helmet-to-helmet hits. And when a player goes down hard, everyone loses their minds.

Coach: "Are you kidding me?"

Parent: "We got that on tape!"

Coach: "You didn't see that helmet-to-helmet?"

Me: "It's called football."

After the game:

Parent: "You've got a flag. Use it so kids don't get hurt!" Me: "He can play volleyball next year."

It's a contact sport. Someone's going to get hurt. You can water it down all you want, but there's always that one kid who takes it too far. That one coach who's looking for an edge.

I once threw a flag during an injury timeout because a player said, "We've taken him out. Now let's take out the quarterback."

Coach: "He didn't mean it."

Parent: "How can you throw a flag when nothing's happening?"

Another Parent: "Told you he didn't like us!"

Parent: "That's just BS. Throwing flags for no reason!"

Parents don't hear the trash talk between players on the field, especially during rivalry games. One team comes out of a blow-up tunnel. The other team blasts music, and they meet at midfield and start yelling, not to play, just to show off.

High school game times vary by state. Most start on time. But some run five to ten minutes late. Teams are supposed to be on the field ten minutes before kickoff. So why do some states let teams go back inside and come out thirty seconds before kickoff? I hate that. We officials just stand there awkwardly staring at each other like we're waiting for a bus. A game should run on a tight schedule.

7pm – is game time

5pm - officials arrive at the game

5:15pm - officials walk the field

6:15pm - officials take the field

6:50pm – band plays National Anthem

6:55pm – coin toss

7pm – kickoff

9:00 – 9:15pm game over

If every game could run this smooth!

TEN

Officials can call a penalty on every single down in football. They can make a ghost foul appear in basketball. And in baseball, a strike can magically become a ball. That's the power of the whistle, the flag, or the click of a counter. But just because we *can* make a call doesn't mean we *should*.

In football, you can wave off a flag depending on the situation. The scenario matters. For example, holding at the point of attack is a big deal. Most of those calls come from the wings or the umpire. Holding during a pass play? That's usually the downfield judge's territory. But here's the thing, downfield judges have a disadvantage. They can't always see in front of or to the side of a player, so most of their calls have to be obvious. We're trained to look for advantages or disadvantages. If the arm is bent, you've got nothing. But if the arm is locked out straight, now we're talking offensive or defensive pass interference.

Each downfield judge is assigned one player to watch. But sometimes, you get what we call ball hogging, officials looking out of their zone, trying to make a call that isn't theirs. Coaches love to gamble and throw the ball deep, hoping for a flag. What they don't understand is that it all comes down to angle and judgment. Most of the time, we let the players play. But there's always that one guy who gets beat and grabs a jersey or an arm. If the wing official sees it from behind, he might not throw the flag because it's not in his zone. The downfield judge, meanwhile, is in front of the play and can't see the jersey being pulled from behind. So no flag. And the coach loses his mind.

Coaches always want a number. "Who was it?" they yell. Sure, sometimes we can give one, like on a facemask. You see the pile, the head twist, and then you've got to trace the hand to the arm to the jersey to the number. Most of the time, we just pick a number and keep the game moving. Coaches yell for flags like they're ordering off a menu.

Now let's talk basketball. You blow your whistle, and you better have a foul, or be ready to make one up. We call those anticipation fouls. Once that whistle blows, there's no taking it back. A slight touch, a brush, an illegal screen. It can all be a foul depending on how the game's going. Reffing a lopsided game is brutal. You see so many fouls, but you let them go just to get the game over with. But there's always that one coach who wants every single call made.

I had a basketball game once; the score was 55 to 7. A player traveled, and I didn't blow my whistle.

Coach: "You're just going to let him travel and not call it?"

Me: "Did he gain an advantage?"

Coach: "No, but it's still a rule."

Me: "He traveled and then lost the ball out of bounds. No advantage gained, so I let it go."

Coach: "But how's he supposed to learn if you don't call it?"

Me: "Fair point. I'll start calling it both ways."

Five minutes later—

Coach: "Okay, let them play."

Me: "What are we teaching them if we don't make the call?"

Coach: "Well, I'll keep my mouth shut and let you do your job."

You can never please a coach.

Now, baseball. You get in position and make the call. Depending on which way it goes, a coach might come out and give you grief. You never know what's going on in his life. Maybe his job's on the line. Maybe his wife is threatening divorce. When I do AAU baseball, some coaches act like they're managing in the big leagues. They sit outside the dugout, giving the catcher signals like they're calling pitches in Game 7 of the World Series. Really? Just get the ball across the plate.

At the younger levels, pitchers don't have control. They don't know what an inside curveball is. What really gives me a belly laugh is when the youth league catcher calls timeout, walks to the mound, and covers his mouth with his glove like he's on national TV. There are sixty cameras in the MLB. There are zero at a 10U AAU game. Even in high school, you see it, like the game's being televised.

When the ump is behind the plate, the catcher's job is to protect him. No balls should hit the ump. From there, we know how to call balls and strikes. And let me tell you, games move fast when pitchers just throw strikes. That's all we want. Get the ball over the plate, and let's play ball.

You've got to remember, kids are out there to learn the game and have fun. That's the heart of it. They should be running hard, getting tired, and going home ready to sleep like a rock. Sure, extra practice is great. It helps them sharpen their skills and understand the game better. But at the end of the day, it's about balance. Let them enjoy the process, grow through the effort, and fall in love with the game not just the grind.

ELEVEN

Adult leagues are where you, as an official, either move up or stay put. I've only worked baseball and football in the adult leagues, and let me tell you, it's a whole different world.

In baseball, players range from 19 to, well, whatever. The oldest I've seen was 53. He was the pitcher. Wow. Just wow. He lasted two innings. By then, the score was 11–0 after walking six batters and giving up three home runs. He was cooked. His fastball had no gas, his change-up was just "change," and his curveball hit the dirt and bounced over the plate. When he walked off, he mumbled, "I'm having a bad day." No kidding.

The first two years were great. After that, it became the same old routine, guys trying to relive their glory days. A lot of wannabe pros. The pace was fast, and the trash talk was nonstop. Cussing was allowed, but no F-bombs. Of course, a few slipped out.

My all-time favorite game. A guy brought his girlfriend to the game. I was the base ump. She got into it— trash-talking him and his buddies like she was the team's hype woman.

Girl: "What in the hell, you bring me to a game to relive your younger days?"

Guy: "Chill out, babe. We're just here to have a little fun."

Girl: "You even have real umps here?"

Guy: "Just watch the game, babe."

Girl: "Hey ump, how'd they get you to come have fun?"

Me: "I get paid to do this." Girl: "Honey, do you get paid to do this?"

Guy: "No."

Girl: "So you're wasting my time just so you can have fun?"

Guy: "Babe, come on, you're embarrassing me."

Girl: "The ump's the smart one, he gets paid to babysit y'all. I got out of bed for this crap. Scott, you need to pay me to leave, or I'll keep talking!"

She made me laugh throughout the game.

Before every adult baseball or football game, I'd gather the team captains and give them my pregame talk. After we officials were paid, I'd say, 'Captains, I am Mr. Roarke. Welcome to Fantasy Island!' Because let's be honest, most of them were out here trying to live out a fantasy.

Adult football was a whole different beast. These guys showed up wearing gear I hadn't seen since my old sandlot days, mismatched pads and jerseys that looked like they'd survived a garage sale. And the phrase of the day? "Back in the day." I must've heard that a thousand times.

There was cussing all around, and the F-bomb was flying around.

One coach called a timeout and started drawing up a play on the ground like we were back on the playground. I blinked, trying to make sense of it. These guys paid to try out, paid to play, and that's how we officials got paid.

Trash talk was top-tier.

Player A: "I bought new cleats because I burned the others running past defenders last week."

Player B: "I'm gonna be your shadow today, I'll be all over you."

Player A: "Heads up, the ball's coming to me."

Player B: "Cool. I'll take it back for a pick-six."

Quarterback got sacked. Running back chimed in: "Back in the day, I ran for five touchdowns and 200 yards." These guys would run one or two plays and then need oxygen.

Most games were played at high schools or playgrounds. One game in DC was half baseball field, half football field, all artificial turf. Somebody must have known somebody. That field was nice. The players? Not so much. Out-of-shape men questioning every flag. Explaining the rules got repetitive. The chop block was the one rule nobody understood. One offensive player blocks high, another blocks low on the same defender. That is Illegal every time.

I've talked to officials who still do adult leagues. The war stories are wild. Teams argue with each other. Not enough players. A few guys said they played college ball and were just trying to stay in shape. But every game had two or three injuries.

One game, a player broke his leg.

Player A: "It's broken... it's broken!"

Player B: "Is there a doctor out here?"

Player C: "Oooooo, man, that looks bad."

Player A: "Give me a cigarette."

Player C: "I got some weed in the car."

Player A: "Bring that too."

Coach: "I called for the ambulance."

Player D: "Can he move off the field so we can finish the game?"

Player A: "Did someone get that weed?"

Five minutes later, the ambulance showed up. Ten minutes after that, he was gone. The game was in the fourth quarter with four minutes left. Score was 28–7. They called it quits.

To think that some of these guys play without insurance. Like I said, there were two to three injuries per game. One guy told me he was unstoppable "back in the day."

Player: "Bruh, I was the man. Colleges were looking at me."

Me: "Nice. Must've broken some records."

Player: "Pro scouts are looking at me now." I looked around and saw maybe ten people there.

Me: "They must've missed this game."

Player: "There's one or two here."

Me: "How old are you?"

Player: "Twenty-five. I look young for my age." He was really 34.

Me: "You don't say. But you haven't played yet."

Player: "Coach is keeping me fresh for the second half."

He finally got in on a punt return, ran it back three yards, and ran out of bounds.

Adult football started getting old for me. There was too much complaining and too much nonsense. Players were always ready to fight and had zero respect for the game and each other. It was unorganized and chaotic. Sometimes, teams didn't even have enough players. I've seen only eight guys show up. Then they'd start calling friends to come play. Game time was 1:00, but the kickoff didn't happen until 2:15.

One time, a coach had to suit up and play quarterback until the real QB arrived.

During a game, I was the deep judge on the sideline. I was running backward, tripped over a helmet, did a full backward roll, and popped back up like nothing happened. Got a good cheer from the players for that one.

I lasted six years in the adult league. Those games will toughen you up mentally, emotionally, and sometimes physically. Nobody really knew the NFL rulebook, and honestly, we didn't either. We just winged it. If we said it was a rule, it was a rule. Rule interpretation wasn't a big issue because, well, we were the interpreters. The game clock? That stayed on the field with us. We ran it how we liked. If the vibe said five minutes left, that's what it was. If the vibe said, "let's wrap this up," then guess what, two-minute warning came early.

The money was so-so. Started at $100 a game, eventually bumped up to $150. I laugh every time someone says they play semi-pro. Reminds me of the movie *The Longest Yard.*

At those games, it was mostly coaches and players fussing about calls. Not too many fans showed up. It was usually just girlfriends and kids. The most I ever saw at these games was about 50 people.

One time, a player slipped down the sideline on a punt return and made it to the end zone. But the referee was standing right there and said he stepped out. Oh, that player went off and called the ref every name in the book. That score would've tied the game—with 30 seconds left. But hey, we got out without working overtime.

TWELVE

This high school has 18 state titles and has sent plenty of players to Division I colleges. Their QB wins three state titles in a row, and he got offers across the country. At least a dozen went into the NFL, and even a Hall of Famer. This is just one high school in that area.

A high school football team wins two state titles with the same quarterback. Then that QB goes Division II. That should tell you something about the talent pool in that state.

Parents always have high expectations for their kids, and I get it. They've invested in shoes, trainers, travel teams, private coaches, and highlight reels. They want a return on that investment. But talent is everywhere, and not every kid is going DI.

When the DI letter doesn't come, it's off to DII, DIII, or junior college. And that's when you hear the fallback line: "Well, it's a free education." Sure, it's free. But we're not talking about *FREE EDUCATION,* we're talking about talent.

I've seen some McDonald's All-Americans. And I've seen players who *think* they're McDonald's All-Americans but couldn't even make the Wendy's All-American team. Get your free education, yes, but what the kid does with it is what really matters.

If you're gifted enough to go pro, it usually shows early. You see it in the teens. You might dominate your local area, but put that on a national scale and it's a whole different game. There are 255 Division I football programs, 167 Division II, 250 Division III, and 65 junior college teams. Only about 2% of players from DII or DIII ever make it to the pros. So, when parents start smack-talking officials about how their kid's going DI, we take note. Because to get there, you need more than hype, you need skill.

What are coaches and parents teaching these 8–14-year-old travel teams across all sports? Because once those kids hit high school, the NFHS isn't going to tolerate spoiled attitudes, taunting, or drama. My personal prediction? By 2030, we'll have traveling high school football and basketball teams. It's already heading that way.

And in professional sports, talent alone isn't enough. Success depends on chemistry, attitude, and work ethic. You can be the most gifted athlete on the field, but if you're a locker room nightmare or allergic to hard work, you won't last.

While you may not have witnessed unruly behavior at your local youth football or basketball games, it's a widespread issue nationwide. Unruly parents, coaches, and friends are negatively impacting the youth sports experience across every sport and level.

It's not just about respect—self-pride and dignity go a long way when it comes to teaching today's youth. Good sportsmanship isn't just a handshake at the end of the game; it's a reflection of character. Sure, everyone wants to win, but someone's going to walk away without the trophy. That's life. Learning how to lose with grace is just as important as learning how to win with humility.

And when you step into the role of an official, it's a gut check. This gig isn't for the weak, the timid, the thin-skinned, or the shy. You've got to be sharp, confident, and ready to take heat from all directions. Honestly, it's tougher than getting chewed out by a drill sergeant on your first day of boot camp. At least the sergeant eventually stops yelling. Coaches and fans? Not so much.

.

Conclusion

As I reflect on my journey as a sports official, I am reminded of the countless moments that have shaped my understanding of the game and the people involved. From the early days of youth leagues to the high-stakes environment of high school, college, and semi-pro games, each experience has been a valuable lesson in patience, resilience, and the importance of fair play.

Officiating is not just about enforcing rules; it's about fostering a spirit of sportsmanship and respect among players, coaches, and fans. The challenges and confrontations I've faced on the field have taught me the significance of maintaining composure and integrity, even in the most heated situations. It's a role that demands unwavering dedication and a deep love for the sport.

Officiating teaches you patience, resilience, and how to stand your ground when the crowd's roaring and the coach's arms are flailing like he's starring in a musical. You learn to read the room, not just the rulebook. You learn that good sportsmanship isn't just for players, it's for coaches, parents, and yes, officials too.

You see the best and worst of people on the field. You see kids learning life lessons, adults refusing to grow up, and coaches trying to balance ego with leadership. You see talent, heart, and sometimes just pure comedy. And through it all, you keep the game moving, keep the peace, and keep your dignity even when you trip over a helmet and roll back into position like a ninja.

Answer to Questions

1) True

2) True

3) False

4) True

5) False

6) True

7) False

8) True

9) False

10) False

9 781970 378566